First published in the United Kingdom in 2015 by
Pikku Publishing
54 Ferry Street
London E14 3DT
www.pikkupublishing.com

ISBN: 978-0-9928050-4-3

Text and Illustrations © Markus Majaluoma
Original title: Hulda kulta, tästä pääsee rannalle!
First published in Finnish by Werner Söderström Corporation (WSOY)

Cover design: Glyn Bridgewater
Translated by Anja Leppanen

1 3 5 7 9 10 8 6 4 2

Printed in China by Toppan Leefung Printing Ltd

Daisy Darling, Let's Go to the Beach!

A Daisy and Daddy Story Book
Vol. I

MARKUS MAJALUOMA

Pikku Publishing

00759796

It is morning.

The sun is high in the sky and soon

everyone is feeling hot.

Daddy takes a look out of the window.

'Daisy darling, let's have a jolly day on the beach!

Do you remember where you put the spades

and other beach things?'

Yes, Daisy does remember.

The bicycle is such a fine invention!

Overtaking everyone, you can find the best spot

on the beach.

'Hey, it's that way!' says the seagull.

Oh, bother, on the beach the bicycle is not

such a good idea.

But the dog thinks that a proper sand bath

is just the thing. Brrrr!

Woof, woof! The dog welcomes his new friends.

The new friends find a good spot under the tree.

'Daisy darling, could you spread some

suntan lotion on my back?' Daddy asks.

Daisy fills the yellow spade.

'Look, Daisy! I've cut a slice of watermelon.

It looks just like the mouth of a whale. Yum, yum!'

Daddy tries to scare Daisy.

But Daisy is not afraid of whales or anything.

She runs to the shore to watch the fish.

Daisy pokes a big fish with a stick.

It is beautiful.

'Do you want the fish?' a fisherman asks.

'As you are so nice, you can have it.'

Daisy looks for a home for the fish.

The floral hat of a lady is just right.

There the fish sparkles like a golden

statue in the middle of a park.

'What has four letters and lives in the sea?'

the lady asks.

'Fish', Daisy whispers in the lady's ear.

'Correct! What a fine, clever girl you are!'

Daisy runs to the kiosk.

'Would you like an ice cream?'

the ice cream man asks.

'Here you are, you good little girl.'

The lady also wants an ice cream.

She is feeling a little poorly.

'Why does the beach smell so terribly

of herrings?' she wonders.

Daisy meets an old crab on the sand.

Would he like an ice cream?

Ouch! The ice cream falls on the head

of the crab.

Mr Crab has had enough of beach life for one day.

Daisy runs after the crab to the water. But oh!

The waves are so large that only crabs dare to

go swimming.

Daisy notices children on the beach.

'Hi there! Aren't sand blankets amazing?'

'Everyone should always make sand blankets!'

Then Daisy gets an idea.

The sun goes down.

Daisy's hard work is done.

Daddy gets a fright.

Suddenly he thinks that he is in the stomach

of a whale.

'Help! I'm inside a whale!'

The lifeguards dig Daddy out

with Daisy's big, red spade.

Then they try to pick the grains of sand off his back.

'If Sir must use so much suntan lotion,

it becomes impossible to remove all the sand!'

On the way home, Daddy pedals fast.

'Didn't we have a jolly day at the seaside?'

he puffs.

Daisy, too, is happy because Daddy's

back is covered with many exciting

sea creatures.